I, Siglavy

ᘁ ᘁ ᘁ ᘁ ᘁ

LISBETH ASAY

XENOPHON PRESS

Available at www.XenophonPress.com

Published by Xenophon Press LLC
7518 Bayside Road, Franktown, Virginia 23354-2106, U.S.A.
xenophonpress@gmail.com

Cover photo of Siglavy Sagana II by Sally Barnett, 1983, at Stonehenge replica in Maryhill, Washington. Back cover photo by Sally Barnett

ePub edition:

ISBN: 9781948717007

Print edition:

ISBN: 9780933316881

Dedicated to all the animals
we share this world with

Chapter 1

U U U U U

Tuesday, September 16

In September in Oregon, on some days, everything seems a bit dazed from living the summer so intensely. The trips are taken, the juicy grass and berries eaten. Last winter is forgotten, the coming of a new one not yet felt.

On such a day, I felt the sharp claws in my stomach for the first time. Margaret was feeding dinner in the barn. Of course I saw she noticed when I tried to escape the pain by moving around instead of standing still, staring at her, as usual, wanting her to serve me my hay first. I saw the look in her eyes, when, after feeding, she called the veterinarian who came quickly, listened to my belly, did the rest of the colic procedure and stayed for a while. The claws loosened their grip and I relaxed.

By now I knew it was the black cats sharpening their claws by tearing at my intestines. I could have gone at that first encounter; but how could I leave her alone with that look in her eyes? I had seen it before, but not caused by me then.

"Keep an eye on him," the vet said to Margaret when she left. I did feel better that evening. I even relieved myself, but I didn't feel like eating.

I had been with my son Chaser in the fields in front of the house all summer, nuzzling, fidgeting, and grooming over the fence. We had just moved to the back fields beside the barn. So I padded about there with Chaser, nipped at the grass, without really eating, pleading for time, even though that is not how we do it.

I knew Margaret was worried. I wasn't. I just needed a little time, even after all these years since I first got to know her.

Back then, I had also felt a change coming: The other animals disappearing from my man Don's barn, one by one or whole groups at a time. The elephants going I didn't mind. It is not that they bother anyone, but they...well...I, Siglavy, I am the king of flight, and they don't even notice. The camels going I didn't mind either, haughty creatures. But it hurt to see the other horses led out of the barn and then hearing the big cars start up, until the only ones left were the black horse, the Andalusian, and me, the Lipizzaner.

We knew something was up. The ever-emptying stalls; all the mares gone. I was waiting for the signal to play, but it didn't come. Don, my man, was silent. Every time he passed my stall I asked loudly, but he just patted me or gave me a treat. But I didn't need a treat. I needed to play, or perform. He tried to hide it, but I could sense it, a dark cloud in his head, a smell of illness seeping out of his body. He tried to pretend he was as before, strong, but of course I knew he was getting weak. He was a good man, quiet with his words, clear in what he was showing me.

6

I knew from the different tents we used to pass through that not everyone's person was a good one. Some were into domination. I saw it in the other horses' eyes, and I smelled it from their bodies, this scent of underlying anxiety. Others were into conversation. My man Don was into soft words and gentle touches.

Sometimes I was alone on stage with Don on my back. I danced to the music. When I lifted my legs higher than usual to the pressure of his legs against my ribs, half closed my eyes and turned slowly, people said they had never seen a prettier waltz. And then, when we came charging, four stallions, into the arena one by one, galloping, free, the audience gasped and clapped. I entered first, since I was the leader of the stallions. Don said I was the best lead horse he ever had. I looked to Don for my cues while the other horses kept their eyes on me.

We were in many circuses, always traveling, always moving. I had to learn to trust Don also with the big cats. In the beginning, it was hard. Don led me alongside their wagon once a day; it reeked. I trembled and just wanted to spin around and fly. But when we were safely past the wagon, Don gave me a treat and I felt good again.

Fear has many faces. Sometimes it shows itself as a wave that hits you and crashes into your body, paralyzing it. This is the dangerous fear because the cause of it will either pass you by or kill you. Other times fear comes on slowly, through a smell or a sound or a movement, causing us to widen our nostrils, turn our ears, raise our heads, and look around by moving only the eyes.

This is how we are and how we always have been. The survival of the herd depends on the calm leader making the right decision: Run or stand your ground. And the good person knows this and can use it and show us many new things signaled from a discrete hand or body movement that only we notice.

So I had to trust my man's command: "Stay!" although every instinct screamed: "Go!" Don never bolted, and he passed that quietness on to me. I think that saved me the night the new black cat had gotten out of his cage and crept into our stable tent. Everything is first smelled, then it is heard, and lastly it is seen. This is how it is and has always been.

This one cat was hidden by the blackness of the night. I only saw his eyes, yellow, cold, never leaving me, never blinking. I heard him, when he yawned and shifted his body, only a slight rattling of his claws against the floor betrayed him. I think he did that on purpose. That whole night I smelled death, a stench of decaying meat pumped out with his every breath.

I never let him know I was afraid, I never left his eyes alone, I never moved a muscle. I didn't let the fear in, not until morning when they found him and caught him. Then the shaking started, and the sweat broke out and covered my body in foam. This was the only time I saw Don upset, even though he tried to hide it, stroking me, whispering: "I am so sorry, I am so sorry."

After that I couldn't be around black cats, and Don canceled our performance, if they had planned them on stage. He was always loyal to me, Don. Always.

I had that same feeling of loyalty when the woman, I didn't know her name was Margaret then, suddenly stood in front of me in Don's emptying winter quarters. She had a little one in her arms, a boy. I didn't know what to do, so I just went quiet. We were both quiet. I was watching her. She was watching me.

"Who are you?" she seemed to think. I learned later on she couldn't help it. She always asked that because she tried to understand us, to look into us, into our true nature. For a person, she is not big, but swift. She squeals or charges fast towards an unruly colt just like a big mare will do, making him stand still and bow his head in respect.

Every horse gets the same scrutiny from those blue eyes: "Who are you?" And we like it, and respond, in our own discrete equine ways: A glance of fear or of trust; of haughtiness or humility; a flicker of the ears; the shifting of a foot; a tightening or softening of our necks; a neighing; the thin skin above our eyes forming little wrinkles.

My herd was gone. She had a boy in her arms. I adore the little ones. We don't get to father so many in the circus, the demands of the show, I guess. I am born a stallion, a protector of mares and little ones. I knew I could take care of her and her child. I knew even then she was one who knew how to talk to us because I could tell she was safe with me now and surprised by it. Many women back then were not used to stallions, men handled us. I showed her I wasn't like those stallions with their snorting, pride, and feistiness. I could be just like she was then, a little reserved, a little standoffish.

Most people, not her though, think they can understand us but not us them. They think they can hide things from us; they believe we neither have feelings nor can perceive others' feelings. They assume because we don't twist our faces like they do we cannot understand our surroundings. We can.

They read letters, we read Nature. Nature speaks all the time in all her creations, who all have a different language. More than most, I like to read that language. I think maybe that was my special gift that the circus had perfected in me. I really like to look at each of Nature's species and members, except the big black cats, of course, and ask: "Who are you?" Then they freely show me just who they are. You can feel it, you know, exuding out of a being, people included: kindness, unrest, fear, curiosity, hatred, meanness, openness, interest. It is all there, plain as day to read.

She stepped closer, and soon she was standing right in front of me with her squirming baby boy in her arms.

"Yes," I said to my man Don: "Get her." I tried to convey this without her noticing. I knew she had sharp powers of observation. But still, they are slow sometimes. It has to go through so many muddy channels with them. It is not like with us, a sharp image suddenly there. Like now, I saw us, clearly depicted, a little family, my new herd.

The little one squirmed. I sensed some resistance in the woman. I pushed my man Don harder, finally he got it. He turned to her and said: "You know, Margaret—let's do it like we circus people do it. Take Siglavy home for six months, and if you don't like him bring him back."

Home became here. That is, a place up from where two rivers meet, the Willamette and the Clackamas, before they run into the mighty Columbia, and where there's a waterfall so broad it's next to Niagara in power. By the rivers are trails where Native Americans used to fish for salmon, and where the Stone Age tools were so plentifully strewn around that other people much later would just bend down and pick up bowls and grinders and mortars as playthings for their kids. Traveling steeply upwards through Oregon City one reaches a plateau with rolling fields and groves of trees. From there, on a clear day, Mount Hood, perfect volcanic cone mountain, rises out of the horizon like a shimmering mirage.

Some of the farms here are old, the planks untreated and grey with age, showing their past with silent dignity. Covered wagons from the days of the Oregon Trail stand in front of barns from the early days, without any museum signs, as if the travelers had just stepped down and walked inside. Once in a while a cougar or a coyote will trot by, but always the eagles and the hawks circle above, watching. This countryside, although a bit rugged, is the kind that makes people put down roots and tend their land. It is land populated from old.

I am showing off after arriving! Highland Stables, 1981

Chapter 2

UUUUU

Wednesday September 17

In the early morning, I hear her coming towards me and Chaser. As always, he has a hearty appetite. She calls my name and holds out her hand with grain in it. I eat slowly from her hand. She needs more time.

When I lean my head on her shoulder she lets me nibble at her collar. Then she gently strokes my nose. She has to leave. Horses hungry for breakfast whinny inside the barn, where, instead of Italian tiles on the floor, there are little clusters of cobwebs in the corners. No bronze heads mounted above the stall doors here. Instead the heads of live horses lean out, softly greeting whoever wanders in.

There is always a gentle wind flowing through. The air feels good, not too warm, not too cold. The indoor arena has soft footing, with a newer addition of a small arena with a roof and high walls for concentration, perfect for lunging and circle work. I like that.

At the base of the stairs up to the viewing room, on the right side, two slightly uneven lines are drawn almost parallel. Underneath them are written, in a childish hand: John. Above them: Tricia.

UUUUU

My nibbling on Margaret's collar has let my mind remain in the night's dreamy state, allowing it to drift back to when I found her. Actually I found her husband Greg first. Greg and Margaret made handmade horse tack, and Greg was often on the road selling their products. He came upon my man Don on one of those business trips. You see, my man Don, besides training animals, also made and sold harnesses, but solely to circus people and magicians' shows.

The truth was, my man Don was ill and needed a home for us. So he showed us to Greg. Us, that is, his three remaining stallions, who came into the arena one by one when he called us by our names. Yes, I remember that moment well when Greg first met me. There was something in his eyes. Greg had also been ill. On the road selling handmade horse tack, he had been hospitalized with an aneurysm in the brain.

"He wasn't himself for two years," is all Margaret ever said about it. So I can only wonder how it was for a young Scottish woman to bear this, alone with her six year old son in the countryside in a foreign country. The dream of an adventurous spirit, living with horses on a little Western ranch, as countless immigrants before her had done, had turned into a nightmare.

With a child and horses to take care of, the stables so close Margaret could hear them snorting from her kitchen window, and her husband and business partner ill, she turned to what she knew from the old country: Thoroughbreds. She found them at the racetrack in Portland, turned them into eventers or jumpers, sold them, and stayed on the land till Greg's health returned.

So when I met Greg, in his eyes I saw life and fun and circus…and myself: I, Siglavy, the most splendid gift a man with a new chance on life, and another boy just born, could buy his horse-crazy wife. And when Don McLennan said he bred me for five hundred dollars per breeding, Greg saw a way to pay for me. When he went home he told his wife to go and see me. That was how I found Margaret.

Most people are not aware that the instinct that makes them look for the right one among other people is also taking place within the animal kingdom. We, the animals, look for the right one among you people. I will admit, though, humans do at times search for the right one among the animals too, but not as often as in the old days when people had spirit animals and painted us on their cave walls.

People of today have forgotten much. Yet, when found, this connection between human and animal can lead to a strong bond, or love as they call it, as strong or in many instances stronger than between two people. As lovers seek each other, so animals also seek their mate from the world of people. Why, I don't know, but then, what do we know of how things really are? Where does the bond between the world and its creatures really come from? All I know is that I had found my Margaret, and I had to take care of her.

During the first winter in my new home here at Highland Stables, I was always wet, either from sweat or from rain. We never sweated in the circus. Our performances only lasted minutes and consisted of a few steps executed under roofs. What if someone from the circus had seen me then? The master of liberty work, sweating at the end of a lunging rope, in the rain, short of breath, getting my white legs muddy? What would they have thought?

Then she wanted me to jump over poles. I am an artist, not a trained poodle. I couldn't make myself do it. I still had my manners, though, and I wasn't about to lose them, whatever she put me through. Eventually, I realized it was possible to canter up to the jump looking eager to go over it. Then, when I dipped my head and twisted my behind, I upset the balance, and a rider not as expert as she would fall off. She never fell off though, so I didn't feel I put her in any danger. She never got upset, either. She just kept at it, as if to see who was more stubborn.

I didn't really understand what we were doing until we entered the three-day eventing competitions: One day in an arena doing dressage patterns, one day out on trails galloping over jumps and water, and one day jumping inside an arena. This kind of horsemanship had just become popular in Oregon, and people from all over moved here to take part. By that time I had gotten in shape to gallop across the countryside. Tiny Margaret made me, only 15 hands tall, look enormous. The only thing familiar to me in this kind of performance was hearing the roar of the crowd, almost as in the circus, as we flew over huge logs, my long white mane and tail waving in the air. However, that was yet to come.

Margaret and I are jumping on
the cross country course at an event.
Photo by Mary Cornelius, 1983

Forgive an old horse for getting lost in time, now that there is so little left of it. When I first came here, I had too much time. I had a warm stall, good food and my own field, but there was no more traveling, no work except for the grueling conditioning work. It was quiet here.

This quiet allowed me to dwell on Don, my man. I had been with him for six years, since I was a mere colt of three. He came by my new home sometimes, either with a monkey, a giant parrot, or one of those insufferable camels, claiming he was on the way to some performance. I knew, of course, these were excuses. He was coming to see me and how I was doing.

As he had always done, he let me stand by his side and suck on his collar. This is something that has always given me the deepest peace of mind. In this state, I could tell him how wet I got, and how I missed him, and how sad I was to feel his strength wane. I told him how I mourned the fact that the day would soon come that I would not see him again.

Every time he came I did this, until one day I heard him tell Margaret: "You know, you could build an indoor arena. It is not that difficult. I did it with the help of my elephant." Don kept prodding her, until I saw my new indoor arena, quite a luxury in Oregon then, starting to come up. It even had a new barn with 12 stalls attached to the side.

$$\cup\cup\cup\cup\cup$$

The last time I saw my man Don, he came by and asked Margaret if he could borrow me for a magician's show in Portland. He also asked if she wanted to come along and learn how to make a lot of money in a few minutes. There were some difficulties in the beginning, black cats of course, which were to be on stage before us. This caused Don to talk sternly to the arrangers to have the cats removed. Despite this, it promised to be a really nice outing for all of us; and I looked forward to impressing Margaret.

The hall, Arlene Schnitzler's, had a scene close to the sloping red velvet covered seats, and balconies overhead, and colored glass in windows and lamps and a little over the top decorations on the walls. It made me feel very much at home, my circus blood pulsing again.

We were waiting behind the stage for our turn, when suddenly one of the heavy stage curtains came down. Not slow and controlled, no: It fell from the sky, crashed like thunder and hit the floor, causing many to scream and run away. But not Don. He just stood there, so I just stood there too. Then we did our wonderful performance. I waltzed with Don on my back and did a little dance completely on my own, to which the audience gasped and clapped. But all Margaret talked about afterwards was how only a little ripple on my skin betrayed the slightest apprehension from the thunderous curtain.

After this, Margaret made me a circus outfit of patent blue leather that she dyed herself. My man Don had taught her how to cue me for my bows and my high-stepping Spanish walk, as well as my liberty work, where I trotted and cantered around her without reins. Margaret wore a white cowboy hat and white pants, and a pair of cowboy boots she had colored blue. My leather boots were blue, too. She made them for me so that my hooves would not damage the floor in the gymnasium at the school in Beaver Creek. That was our first little performance, and the audience was beside itself with enthusiasm. From there, we started to travel up and down the West coast. The whole family came along, and often other Lipizzaners and their people joined us to promote the Lipizzaner breed. I gave my circus routine as proof of our many talents. For years, we did that little act to all kinds of audiences.

Once, in Hood River, on a windy day, we had a big Lipizzaner demonstration beside the Columbia River. The windsurfers on the river moved so fast on the water, their sails taut and bulging in the strong wind. I had to read Margaret's hand signals because the wind carried off all sounds. Some of the other horses got frightened by the wind and the sails. I watched the sails move across the water. I felt just like the surfers, felt the harmony of the movement in hot gusts of wind, in a world without sound, only wind and water. Water and wind, harmony in motion, nothing else.

I am trying on the circus outfit of blue patent leather
Margaret made for me. Photo by Margaret Gill,
Highland Stables, 1982

Chapter 3

Thursday September 18

The mares wander slowly around grazing. I follow them with my eyes. They like to feed at night and rest in the day—when the black cats sleep.

There is a black cat in the barn. He is of the tiny ones, but still, he is one of them. He goes after the little scurrying creatures with hairless tails; with cold and piercing eyes he taunts and torments them until he gets bored and eats them. He looks up at me as he crunches the little bones between his jaws. It sends shivers through all of me, because I know the soul of the cat and all his bigger kind. They want to tear and rip and chew before they slowly lick the blood away from their lips.

On this night, I am alone and the cats are nowhere to be seen, as they would send shadows everywhere. The moon is at its biggest now, when our hair coats soon will grow thicker, and the sweet juicy grass of summer wanes and starts to taste of thinness and cold.

The night doesn't get dark. I can see the mares and the foals, at a distance, grazing and snorting. They have all been difficult in the days leading up to the big moon. It pulls heavy on them, maybe even more than on me. They get flighty and high strung and quarrelsome.

When the moon is at its fullest that tension snaps like the sharp crack of a whip. Their eyes glaze over, and they sigh as they graze in the night. I am drawn to the light in the sky, or rather, it draws me toward itself. It makes me feel good and soft inside. I can bask in the big light from the night sky. I can sink into a comfort in my body, as of coming from a stroking hand or a rare tender nuzzle from a good mare.

On such a night of moons and no black cats, I can dream a little. I can move with the pull of the moon. I can quietly be who I am: A dancer on the shadows of the moon rays.

In the morning, I hear the excited news around the barn that the last mare I bred had given birth to a foal, a colt. This pleases me. I don't like to brag, but when I was 31 years old I heard the vet tell Margaret I had a fantastic volume of live semen. I actually had the ability of a five-year-old stallion.

With the hindsight of old age, I think I now safely can say it was in the first quiet year at Highland Stables that I refined my skills which later gave me my reputation. I was still young and getting in the best shape I had ever been, when they brought the first mare to me. I had time to work on courting, time to get to know her and please her until she willingly came to me.

These are mares, not easy creatures to deal with. Some will be nervous, some will be scared, some will be angry, and some will simply refuse to have anything to do with a stallion. I can understand that. It is nothing personal to me. It is simply a matter of what they have experienced before. Maybe they have no experience at all, and tied up they see an unknown stallion come towards them. I have seen a young innocent filly's eyes widen in horror and her whole body stiffen in fear at the sight. In such a case, most stallions will just move in forcefully.

Not me. I, Siglavy, will gently approach her, nicker softly, get eye contact, hear her answer me, make her relax and trust me. Sometimes, if the mare doesn't show any interest in me, I will just ignore her and graze beside her. This approach can take some time, but I had plenty in those days. The rewards came when, after neighing, nudging and gentle little bites, and of course a little strutting around on my side to show her my genes, my power—I would ask her: "Do you want my foal?" Then, when she willingly surrendered to me I could pass on my genes, my life, my past and start a new life, a future.

It takes all the cycles of the universe combined to get the mare in heat. The moon, the stars, the planets, the wind, the seasons, the shifting of their mysterious minds, but still, it isn't enough. The Lipizzaner mare also has to like her stallion. I have often tried to communicate this to my son Bruce, but he is not listening. He thinks he is irresistible and charges in like a war horse. I have seen him kicked, bitten, or simply rejected more than once.

When Margaret and Greg brought me a Lipizzaner mare for the first time, it was special, like seeing my mirror image in a female. Sadly, we didn't get time to really know each other before this mare got colic and died. The lady who owned her then sent her daughter, Mara, up from

California. Mara was a filly, four years old, about to turn all white, when she became mine.

Most stallions cover the visiting mare, who then disappears, never to be seen again. But I got to see Bruce, and all my foals with Mara, be born, shakily get to their feet, take their first staggering steps, and then discover they can fly over the fields on their spindly legs. Some of them I even got to see turn color. From being born black we gradually change through all imaginable shades of grey, until as adults we turn white.

UUUUU

Everybody needs a job, horses, too; and for many years I had thought my only job was to be a circus horse. Some people despise the circus as vulgar or cheap entertainment. I never saw it as that. To me, circus is a perfectly executed celebration of life, and life a great stage itself. There, I met the most fascinating variety of people and species and skills, also the skills that enabled me to understand others better.

With Sig junior, our first and also the first purebred Lipizzaner foal born in Oregon, I somehow felt I had been given one more job. More than the job of fathering the future, this job also became a job of securing, keeping and improving the past, strange as that may sound.

My offspring were always good; I don't hesitate to say that. Still, I don't know what it was with Mara and me, but the eight foals we had in our life together were exceptional. My mother, Sagana, had been what is called a good mare. However, they said my father, Siglavy Primavera, had a reputation as a very difficult horse to break. But Mara and my foals, they were simply better than us. They became as good as our relatives in the Old Country, as talented as the performers in the Spanish Riding School. I am proud of that.

I still have two of my sons with me, Chaser and Bruce. Chaser is serious and hardworking, Bruce is working hard to avoid the work. It is as if my serious and my funny sides were split in two and each of those two got their half. Bruce is my heir, destined to take over after me, because like me he has the classic baroque look of the oldest purebred horse in Europe.

I can also be funny. I can wriggle my head out of my bridle and I like a joke, but not like Bruce. He tends more towards silly—running off and not letting himself be caught. I would never do that.

My sense of humor is different. It's more like that time a photographer wanted to portray me for a national magazine. Margaret and Greg hauled me up to the Stonehenge replica by Maryhill Museum in Washington while it was still dark. It is such a phenomenal site, perched atop the Columbia Gorge, looking out over green hills and orchards, sloping down to the Columbia river and over to the Oregon side. There, waterfalls thunder down steep cliffs and the mountain sides look like rain forests and strange rock structures are strewn around as by a giant's hand. The grass up there is very sweet.

When the first light emerged they were almost ready to start photographing. I don't mind that. I always liked it, since I can stand still and have them all look at me, and there is always a snack or more afterwards. I was enjoying the sweet grass when two police cars came down the dirt road and stopped by my people. The voices drifting over to me held no meaning: "300 bikers," "annual camp-out," "left a knife-cut body." But the peace of the morning was gone when the cars left and everyone started to move around quickly.

I was trying to detect an unfamiliar odor when the gravel crunched again. I saw a herd of five or six bikes with black clad riders roll slowly towards us. Although no one else was able to, I picked up a whisper of hesitation in Margaret's voice and the slightest slowing down of her step when she told the leader of that strange herd that we would leave soon.

"Yes, even sooner," she said, "if you help us by standing between the columns to block him from running out of the circle."

"If he comes too close, wave your arms," she added. "Just wave your arms."

"Sure, no problem." The leader's voice was bragging, as if I hadn't heard and seen that before from young colts before I put them in their place.

When Margaret let me loose I gave a little extra to my usual hind legs' kick, and at the trot-around-in-a-nice-circle command I gave her my best trot. Each hoof hits the ground with a sharp intention, and powered from behind, I look unstoppable. One leg follows the other in perfect harmony. The rhythm sounds like a wake-up call: One! Two! Three! Four! Run! Laugh! Jump! Dance!

This, I feel, makes most people want to know me better. They tuck in their shirts and straighten their backs. They stand a little taller and step a little higher toward me. They step into my presence.

Not this guy though. As I passed him, I couldn't resist it. I gave him my best hard stare. In return, he looked down and stepped back. And that was when it simply became too tempting. Swiftly, as only I can do it, I turned, gathered all the power of my behind and moved towards him, still in my best trot. Behind me I heard Margaret: "Wave your arms! Wave your arms!"

The guy started shrinking. That's always when fear takes over. As he dove behind the stone, I was outside the circle, galloping up the hill, swishing my tail. From the top of the hill I could see my people, far beneath me. I looked around my new kingdom, stamped my front leg, making the dirt fly, and let out some impressive snorts. Then, it crept up on me that I didn't know where I was. And furthermore, I was alone.

So when I heard Margaret whistle, I don't think anyone noticed, it was in that very moment I decided to turn around and canter back into the safety of the stone circle.

Margaret pointed to where she wanted me: Up on the stone block like a statue! She stepped up first and nudged me to come after. When I was up she took off my halter. Then she stepped down quietly, laid down beside the stone block, hidden from the camera, and said: "Sssshhhh."

I knew what that meant. Stand still. Perfectly still. Perfectly poised for the shot. Perfectly present.

I am posing in the Stonehenge replica, above the Columbia River in Maryhill, Washington. Margaret is hiding behind the stone block I am standing on. Photo by Sally Barnett, 1987, used as a centerfold in the magazine, Horse Illustrated.

See, Bruce, he would never have come back. He would have kept running around, not wanting to be caught, thinking he was being real funny. Chaser, on the other hand, would never have dreamed about leaving the circle in the first place. Although, he might have spun around at full thoroughbred speed, throwing himself up in the air and twisting around so fast as to make those who watched him dizzy. Then he suddenly would stop and quietly come over, asking: "Time for my treat now?" He can't help it, his mother was an English thoroughbred.

I sometimes wonder why Margaret wants to ride such a dangerous horse. Somehow I don't think she ever asks herself that question. Not even way back, as a young woman hired as the groom riding the Master's second horse in the last fox hunt in Scotland. Or even when reading the rules of her workplace, The Lenarkshire and Renfrewshire Foxhounds, which stated: "The Hunt staff are the Masters' personal servants and should not be engaged in light conversation when out hunting."

"Never get between the Masters and hounds. They must always have a clear view of them."

"Always make room for hounds, Masters, huntsman and whippers-in to pass you. In narrow places act quickly and always turn your horse's head towards hounds."

Once she was sent home in shame after a scolding from the Mistress of the Hunt because she had dirtied the Master's reserve horse. It stumbled and fell, tumbling down a steep hillside with Margaret rolling along.

Although the oldest son of that estate was forever locked into a wheelchair after a hunting accident, no one saw this as good reason to quit a tradition upheld by the truly rich and privileged. This is what they did during winter season. They hunted twice a week. It was a full time occupation. In the summer, they did other things. Perhaps recuperating in coastal bath towns?

It was the end of an era. This era had created the English thoroughbred, the cheetah of the equine world, whose every instinct compels it forward, forward, faster and faster. The upper crust in The British Isles must surely have longed for danger when they threw themselves on the backs of these speed monsters, only to be hurled over stone walls and half drowned splashing through creeks before flattening out at dizzying speeds across green fields. Meanwhile, their more sensible aristocratic counterparts on the European continent rode or watched my ancestors executing their highly controlled movements in luxurious riding halls.

Although Chaser is fast, he is also smart and well-behaved like me. He takes his work seriously. But to him the best part of it seems to be before and after-wards. Then he can focus exclusively on being groomed and admired or standing with his nose close to Marga-ret's shoulder while she is talking to someone. He is good looking, strong and poised, with an air of "relax, I'll take care of it" that makes it very pleasant to be around him, also for me. Although, he does embarrass me a bit when he throws himself against the stall door if not greeted properly, or, missing out on a treat, turns around in his stall and sulks with his head in a corner.

These days, these two sons are a great comfort to me. I know Chaser will look after Margaret, and Bruce will make her laugh. Or try to.

At the highest point of my territory there are two gently swaying trees. Behind those two trees is a field with cows, bulls, and calves slowly drifting back and forth, or lying down resting. One of those trees is Mara's. I often look up to her tree, especially now when I know I am soon to join her. A third tree will come up in that peaceful place, where I shall be laid to rest beside Mara, my mare, my companion, the mother of my most gifted children.

Chapter 4

UUUUU

Friday September 19

I often sense people are wrapped in a shroud of former happenings. Here I must insist we are more skillful. They cannot shake off the past like we can. We can walk away from it and into the new moment, which is always waiting, beckoning. I also sometimes wonder if they are aware how time shapes a place, and how, in the quiet of the night, you can see shades and hear whispers and echoes of times gone by. That is, if you listen closely enough.

Sometimes, if I see a shadow of the past in Margaret, I show her one side of me: The archangel blasting out of the sky with head high, nostrils wide, white mane flowing, bulging muscles flexing under shiny white coat. Then I slow down till I float towards her. I stop to bend one knee, stretching the other, thus bowing and inviting her to mount me bareback, pretending I am taking her for a gallop on the beach. This, I know, always makes her smile again.

I wish I could carry her away now, but I don't have the strength this morning for much more than the nibble on her collar and old memories. But how sweet they are. How fresh they seem. So full of life's light and sparkle.

I watch my son, Bruce, patrolling his field at the highest point of the property. He is trotting alongside the fence, showing his body in profile. His legs hit the ground like pounding pistons, his head is turned toward me, neck high.

UUUUU

Last night I dreamed about Tricia. I was in my stall. The light was dim. There were horses around but I couldn't see them, as if they were beyond the reaches of my vision. I only felt them. Then I heard voices, low, almost chanting: "She is here, she is here..." I stood still as I watched a movement in the middle of the aisle. The air in that one spot was moving, getting denser, almost whirling around with some unknown particle until suddenly Tricia appeared, radiant and beautiful. The voices disappeared and Tricia smiled at me with closed lips, as if suppressing a giggle. She has the same fine brown hair as Margaret, but hers is shoulder length, parted at the left side and held up with a red pin. Her eyes are enormous, like her mother's, deep set and blue. Then she darts around the barn helping with chores, all the time talking.

I woke up from the dream, and now I feel dazed, not understanding why I dreamed about the girl who was born into horses. Her grandma called her "our little equestri-enne." At age six, Tricia knew all the horses in the barn, how to clean a stall, how to feed, how to take care of a horse, and of course, how to ride.

Tricia had just gotten a new horse, Fancy Footwork Bucky. Margaret had caught her using the stick too hard on her old pony, expecting too much of him. She then knew Tricia was ready to move on to a more willing ride. That was Fancy Footwork Bucky. Oh yes, he liked to buck, but not viciously, just a little hint when the rider got too demanding, or with too heavy a rider on his back. The girl and that pony fit together so well that Tricia often tried to sneak out of the house, away from her homework, to ride him, telling Martine, the instructor: "Mama said it is OK." Once Margaret had to pull Tricia off the pony. All the people taking lessons heard her screams, demanding to be let back on the horse as she was being dragged across the yard towards the house. She calmed down enough to plead with her mother:

"But I love Fancy."

"Yes, honey, I know you love him. But you have to do your homework. And with Fancy, you have to take your time and really get to know him so you know what is safe to do on him."

"Fancy loves me."

"Yes, yes, he does. Of course he does. But no jumping yet on him. Walk, trot and canter. Then we can start jumping. Remember that horses can hurt, just like people. And since they can not tell us in words, they maybe have to tell us in actions that can kill, like bucking us off."

It was almost show time. That whole week all the young riders were excited. After all the practicing, it was time to bathe the horses, polish the bridles and saddles, and go out in the world to show off their horses and what they had learned. I wasn't going out to a show this time, but the excitement spreads and everyone gets more generous with treats and attention. Tricia was busy too, but she did not forget me as she half skipped, half trotted up and down the aisle. When she was about to pass my stall, I was ready. I bent my head lower and she gave an extra tall skip and her little hand came up and I always managed to catch the treat. If someone saw us and reprimanded her she just looked at me and giggled.

Wednesday night Tricia and Fancy were happy about their lesson with Martine. Thursday she started to get real excited about her very first dressage show. Margaret told her she couldn't ride Friday, since both pony and girl needed to rest before Saturday's show. Tricia accepted that. Also, she had to be home early for a good night's sleep, when she asked if she could go and play with her friend across the lane.

In the middle of that night, the lights came on in the house after Tricia woke up and came crying into her parents' bedroom because her head was hurting so much. That night, fear took hold of all. A fear so violent it vibrated and pulsed through the whole property: Rolling out of the house and slamming into the barn where I, for the only time in my life, gave into it and screamed in anguish. When the helicopter landed and quickly took off, I rammed my body into my door and reared up and tried to jump out.

I never saw Tricia again. They said it was a sudden aneurysm in the brain. I don't know what that is. All I know is Tricia never went to a dressage show and never jumped Fancy because I couldn't protect her when the black cats came to get her.

When the mares lose a foal, they grieve for three days. They call out for the lost little one. They go away from the herd and stand quietly with their head almost down to the ground. They don't eat. But after three days they return to the herd. They start eating. They leave death behind and move into life again. But is it the same life? Have they forgotten? Or do they remember? Do they secretly long for the lost one? Are they forever changed?

Again, the stalls were emptying around me. Margaret's boarders found it all too sad to bear, so they too left with their horses. Didn't they wonder if she, too, wanted to leave: To run back to her homeland? To the sound of her own dialect spoken by others? To the intimacy in handing over of a paper-wrapped packet from the fish monger, whose grandfather she knew all the gossip about? To stop by a childhood friend's house uninvited? To walk along the river Clyde when the snow started falling? And then, did they ask themselves if there really were any old country to go back to? Hadn't life taken its course there too and moved everyone away from a place that once had been? Hadn't all the childhood friends grown up? The Clydesdale horses been replaced by lorries? The fishmongers now behind counters in the supermarkets?

I didn't want to move again. I didn't want to lose Margaret. My hardest job ever started—to bring her back, to keep her with me. She still came to feed me and clean my stall, but that, too, can vanish; that strong tie can snap like thin thread.

Years later she talked to another woman who also had lost a child. The blackness in that woman's sorrow made her unable even to throw her beloved horse some hay. The horse almost died from starvation before neighbors rescued it. Maybe Margaret saw that such a thing is possible, because she started to sell off all her horses. One by one, till it was only me left.

At the end of the night when no one else was up, she came into my stall and let me chew on her collar until she leaned her wet face on my neck. All I could do was to be quiet. When her face was dry I nudged her, more gently than a mare with a newborn foal. When she pulled away from me, her eyes were behind a veil of distance, staring at me from a place unknown, where all is lost, where silence weighs, where questions have no answers. But still, there is dignity; dignity in honor of the child who went away.

Then I nudged her again, to show her the sun had come up, beckoning us to step into its warmth. Slowly. One step at a time. Just one step at a time. Hoping that one day she would want to live again. Not tomorrow. Not in three days. But some day.

Chapter 5

UUUUU

Saturday 20 September

In the summer, we have goldfish in our drinking troughs. They eat the fly eggs. When I dip my mouth in the water I stare into the trough, taking care not to bump into the tiny swimmers. I look at them as I slowly swallow the life giving fluid. They look back at me with their little eyes, which show no fear, no joy, pain or pleasure. But still, they dart away if I move my head and they close in if I am quiet. They make me wonder—is my mouth's submersion in water the most dramatic happening in their life? Are they curious and adventurous? Do they wish for a life outside the drinking trough? A wider horizon?

By now, evening is falling softly. Soon it is dinnertime. The other horses are waiting expectantly. Some can't contain their excitement, but nicker and buck and spin in their fields. Not me. I have neither an appetite tonight nor an urge to run. But I am glad to see Margaret, as she moves from field to field, putting down flakes of hay according to each horse's menu. Some get orchard hay, some need local

hay and the lucky ones gets alfalfa from eastern Oregon,
all according to weight and digestion and work. Now she
is darting around inside the field beside me with her arms
full of hay, searching the ground for a spot without urine or
dung to put it down.

Her whole life is grounded in us. It always was. Long
ago, we drew her into our magical world full of surprises.
A world that gave her courage to live a life she couldn't
have imagined on her own. I often hear her say that all she
wanted was a family. She certainly got that. Her people
family and what we gave her; our ever expanding horse
herd. I will truly say, now that there are not too many things
to be said anymore: It was me who shaped her life. It was
through working with me that she became who she is, a
horse-person. And when the bad times came, it was me who
pushed, pulled, and carried her through to the other side. I
know this, because I, Siglavy, was her mentor in this life.

It might be that it takes three human life spans to
know all about us, to understand us fully and thus become
one with us. What I do know is that there are human babies
born whose pull towards us is one of their first expressions.
Such children see another world. They see a world of adven-
ture, a fairy tale world, a vanished world now suddenly
appearing in front of them. From then on, all they want
is to be part of that world. Some of these children never
let go of us. As adults they live with us. They devote their
lives to know all about us, to work with us and look after
us. Our wellbeing is the very core of their lives, not fame
and fortune, something very few of them ever receive. This
is how riders get the well-balanced, well-behaved horses
they can go out and win ribbons with: This ghost army of
trainers and grooms and stable helpers, always busy in the
background.

Myself, I am drawn to these people who, despite living in this modern and often confusing world, still want to be inside our circle. Some of them have few other people in their lives, either because there is no time left after taking care of us, or, actually quite often, I believe, because they find us more interesting than their own kind. I can understand that.

The day Mike Pereillo came to the barn, I immediately sensed that he was one of those people. Mike had learned our language as a little boy, riding horses that had been moved from the plains' states to be resold in new environments on the east coast. Being taken from the endless rolling peaceful prairies into forested and rocky environments startled them. Like a feral child he spent all day on horseback. His mind started to see exactly what the horses saw. A white tree trunk became a ghost jumping out. A grey rock; a wolf ready to pounce. A paper rustling along the ground or a bird lifting from behind a bush and taking wing was so shocking to the alerted mind of the horse that it wanted to rear and run, causing the boy to sit ever deeper in the saddle, in the quiet of his own mind—so open to the horse's that the frightened animal tuned into it, trusting him that this was not a scary world. No, on the contrary, all was well with the world. All was there to look at and explore. Sometimes to stand still and just see and smell and hear. Other times to run with freedom and the joy of abandonment, in this world of magic that can only live in the minds of animals and children, and sometimes very old people or people of the very old.

I also sensed something lacking. Or rather, Mike had the shroud of the past around him. Something was slightly broken. It took me some time to detect it. It was trust. Trust was broken. Not in us, but in the honor and well-meaning motives of his fellow man. I can understand that. Trust is what we survive by, in the wild and together with people. The leader of the herd is normally a mare, the stallion being the protector; but since my Mara was hopeless as a trusted leader, although a wonderful mother, this job fell on me. I grew used to always being aware, always interpreting my surroundings correctly, so the others never questioned my decisions, never hesitated—but trusted that I did what was best for the herd. If they perceived danger they looked to me for signals. The panicky ones gathered around my calmness, waiting for my signal to run or stand up against the black cats of the world. The colt or filly, who is to learn the way of people, has to carry this trust onward to his or her first trainer in life. If the trainer is good, this bond of trust grows stronger the more we learn.

We haven't always been what we are now. There were times when we lived as free beings. We had our own groups with our mares and our young ones and old ones and our own leaders, but to survive, we had to adapt to the changes of civilization. Some find that easy, others resist.

Sometimes I wonder if this isn't true for many of your people too: To want to be free, to live without the laws and rules of a modern life. Rather than getting to know man's hand or voice, such individuals yearn to gallop in a herd across endless, rolling fields, or drift slowly over them, grazing. If man is to reach the spirit of such creatures, he must see and understand them. Yes, man has to reach into the very bottom of their nature, of their soul, where there dwells a burning longing never to feel a roof over their head, or the taste of metal in their mouth, or tight leather around their belly. Instead, they yearn to roll in warm dust and jump over a stream, to let all senses open fully and take everything in: The warming sunshine, the beckoning moon,

44

the whisper of the grass, the irresistible pull of the endless fields, the unified movement of the herd running. No, it is not so easy to build trust with such ones. It must be proved. It is not a command: "Trust me!" And so it is. No, no, it must be proven over and over again.

But Mike I trusted at first sight. I knew there and then he wanted what was best for us. Only once did I not trust him, and that was a lapse on my part. I am willing to admit that. He had started me in harness and taught me to pull a cart. This was actually great fun, especially when we trotted on the road past the fields, and the horses fled in panic at the sight of the cart. But this day, and I guess he thought I had learned enough so we could travel farther, he pushed me past the property line. I had the blinders on, so I couldn't see behind me or around me, I only saw in front of me. Suddenly I couldn't see my home, my herd, my mares, my Margaret. I was leaving her behind to fend for herself! What if the black cats came while I was gone? I panicked, stood up on my hind legs and spun around, facing homeward. Mike then let me trot towards home, then made me turn nicely around again, and go back and forth within the property line several times, before finally going home. There he told Margaret that maybe pulling a cart wasn't my thing. He was really gentle about it. Although he never told anyone I had panicked and behaved like that, I still cringe when I think about it.

Mike had rented the little barn after the new barn and indoor arena were ready. He came in at six in the morning and fed all the horses. Then he worked with the horses he had in for training, Morgan stallions to be schooled for driving in shows. He was done at noon. Sunday mornings he staged a little show in the arena for the owners, who, eager as parents at school sports, cheered their horses on.

Martine had come some time earlier as a student and boarder. Before she became an instructor, her job was to clean all the stalls, twenty-two of them, put the horses out, and feed them lunch.

UUUUU

In those days, I had a daughter, Kovara. When she was three and a half years old, her coat hadn't started to turn white yet; it was still a light elegant grey. Kovara was slender of build, with a thick, shiny salt-and-pepper mane and tail, and big eyes that looked softly at you, a little sideways, not scared or reserved, just a bit shy. As her father, I was happy to see her start her education under Mike and Margaret. She was used to being handled—groomed and cleaned with water from a hose in the shower stall, and led in a halter in and out from the barn to the fields or the arena. She was thus open to learning more. From now on, new things were asked of her, but only one at a time, like tolerating the feeling of a leather stick rubbed with peppermint in her mouth, and then rewarded. Rewarding is not always a treat. It's also about stopping and allowing a moment to ponder what happened, or to have some quiet and peace and know that this is what the person wanted.

Eventually Kovara was asked to open her mouth and accept a bit of metal, also rubbed in peppermint, several days in a row. When she had learned this, she was asked to try one more thing: Being steered with reins. Mike held the long lines attached to her bridle, walked behind her, and guided her to move and stop and turn from the careful pressure and precise release of the reins. The next piece added was change of gait, to go from stop to walk to trot to walk to stop. She walked so attentively and trotted so exquisitely, like she was taking the utmost care with every step, looking straight ahead with shiny eyes. Her shyness was fading with every session as she gradually became more confident.

Then they put a saddle on her and she was worked in walk and trot with both bridle and saddle. And then, one day when the barn was quiet, the weather good, they decided this was the day for her to feel her first rider.

To begin with, Margaret saddled her and Mike worked her with the long lines, like she was used to. After she had a break and a lot of praise, Margaret settled gently into the saddle. Kovara's eyes widened a bit, her ears picked up, and she shifted the weight on her feet before she let out a sigh of relief. To me, watching from my stall, that said: "No danger, it's just Margaret up there instead of beside me." Then they let her stand and rest and get used to it all before they started her walking, now with a person on her back. Margaret, the live weight, the one new thing added, stayed relaxed and balanced, following Kovara's movements. That day they even trotted! When they finished the ride, Kovara stood still and looked like a well-trained horse, although only moments earlier she had accepted her first rider. It was so smooth, so smooth. But then again, it always was under Mike's hands and voice.

This little routine was repeated every day, ten to fifteen minutes, until it was my turn to take over. I was going to a dressage show, just a small one, not far away, and Kovara was coming with me, to learn from me how to behave in public. When the moment to leave the barn arrived, we had both been groomed until our manes and tails flowed and shone. Kovara followed me, step by step, into the trailer. When she felt the unusual sensation of the trailer moving she stiffened and looked to me, but soon relaxed when she saw I enjoyed being moved by a trailer.

At the show place she followed me a bit timidly and watched Margaret tie me to the side of the trailer and give me hay to nibble; and then the same happened to her, but on the other side. I heard she wasn't eating. That meant she was a little tense while studying her new surroundings, but she relaxed as she heard my calming chewing and sighing. If I spotted a familiar horse or person walking by, she heard my gentle greeting sounds. When I heard her eat her hay, I knew she was fine. Then Margaret came back and groomed, saddled, mounted and warmed up Kovara, same as always. Just like home. Only one new thing added. The warm-up was now beside a dressage arena Kovara had never seen before.

Oh, my grey gorgeous girl, with the silken mane and tail and the slender build! I must admit my heart gave a start when the bell rang, and it was her turn to enter the arena, trot up the centerline and stop midway where the rider greets the judge. The judge returned the greeting and thereby signaled horse and rider to start. Then I sensed apprehension, a slight fear in my daughter's eyes, but only then, because when she moved, it was with precision and grace in every step, oblivious to the judge's scrutiny: Is the circle round? Are the lines straight? How is the transition between the circle and the line, the walk and the trot? Is it smooth? Flowing? What about balance, what about the harmony of the movement?

Horse and rider danced; in an exchange of movement, Margaret followed Kovara, but Kovara also followed Margaret. One led, one followed, and at the same time both moved with each other, so no one could tell who was leading and who was following. When Kovara was done with her three minute performance, her eyes were again sparkling. I still see clearly before me her walk and trot that day, with such a stride, such a pride, as if she said: "Look at me, I am not a filly anymore, I am a mare. I have responsibility. See me! I can dance!"

UUUUU

We are peaceful creatures. We are not driven to hurt anyone or cause pain. We are born like this, and this is how we perceive the world. Not everyone sees the world like this, especially not the black cats, who are born to make harm on such like us. Neither are all people able to fully understand this. I have seen this in my travels, some people hurt us because they don't understand our language. To be honest, I have also seen people who hurt us because they want something for themselves—attention, ribbons, even money. Some people will push us into pain, even death, to obtain this. I cannot understand that.

Although we are born with sharp senses that warn us of others who wish us harm, and thus cause us to run away, we do not express pain well. On the contrary, we are masters of discretion with our own pain. I have seen how dogs show that they hurt, like when I, by accident, stepped on the paw of the barn dog. He howled and yelled and whimpered till everyone came running around! We can't do that. We stumble and won't step down if our leg hurts, but we don't make any sounds. This doesn't mean we don't hurt. An alpha horse can scream as a warning: "Stay away!" Or stallions can scream in excitement. But we don't scream from pain. We try to avoid the pain instead of fighting back.

Long ago, people understood this and made it a foundation of our training. If we can feel and be annoyed by a fly landing and walking on our back, imagine what it feels like to have a person's leg push into our ribs. If we don't do what that leg wants us to do: Yield to it in a lateral, sideways movement, the pressure will become a stronger push. Then maybe a kick, a sting from a whip or a precise and sharp pain from a spur. We try to avoid two legs that apply pressure to our sides by moving forward. Tightening the reins puts pressure on the metal in our mouth. If we don't slow down or stop immediately it will soon hurt.

Reward can thus be cessation of pain, as we surrender to the movement that makes the pain go away. This, most of us learn quickly. And soon only a hint of what initially caused the pain makes us stop, move forward, sideways, faster or slower. That is if we are lucky, if we are among people who understand our pain threshold. This is not always evident but can be seen in a faraway look in our eyes. It can be found in a nervous chewing, a grinding of teeth, or maybe a tightening of the nose.

Rarely have I met aggressive horses. The few times I have, they had become like that from being pushed too far or handled by the wrong person. Not a horse person. We feel strongly about that word. A horse person is a human who understands the mind and the language of the horse. It goes without saying they are rare creatures.

I lie down a bit and rest. I can see the stars, and their silence touches me. I, who never was concerned with time, but lived in the moment, have suddenly got so much time, and such a sense of it. This is peculiar because I know for a fact that my time has run out, but still it is as if I have been given all the time I need. My whole life is coming toward me. Everything I have done, all that I have seen, it all appears to me in such a clear and intense light. It is almost like a wholly new life is given me, but it is coming out of the old one.

And now they are pouring in, all the people I met, all the fun I had, all the performances and the admiration I received. Nowadays it is easy to forget how unusual I was in Oregon back then, a white Lipizzaner stallion, beauty unsurpassed, superbly behaved. In those days of me being an ambassador for my kin, we traveled a lot, showing off how much I knew—circus, jumping, dressage—in all kinds of big horse expositions, meeting interesting horses and their people. Many were drawn toward me, some of them with big names, some of those even told Margaret what a good horse she had.

These memories glide by, and what is left is not the many occasions I got something, praise, applause, treats. No, left with me are the moments when I gave something, however little. As when I gave ten-year old children their first canter, slow, floating, aerial—and felt their trust, even if their balance wasn't so good and I could have let them fall, but I didn't. Or all the people I met who are afraid of animals. With them, I waited patiently till they reached out a slightly trembling hand, which I then gently sniffed, making them smile—making them take their first little step of trust towards me.

All the hands that reached out towards me through the years, I could have avoided or been cranky and turned away. Maybe nipped at a finger if it didn't offer a carrot. But no. I let them pet me even if some didn't know how, but slapped me rather than stroked me, yes, even if they disturbed my midday nap. All these hands I now feel so tenderly stroking me. These moments of others' happiness are now so strong in me that they have become my own happiness.

Chapter 6

Monday September 22

I am happy to see this morning. I wasn't sure it would come. Last night started with a promise of being long, with pains and aches interrupted by dozing. As I stood in the cool autumn night, under stars and moon, over earth and grass, firmly anchored in my knowledge of who I am, suddenly, for some reason, I didn't know whether I was airy spirit or firm matter. I wondered if I was both, or if I had been matter long enough, and now the spirit wanted all of me. These thoughts frightened me and I stiffened. I, Siglavy, froze in fear.

Then, standing there in my field, I saw a mist seeping toward me, slowly, out of the night, out of the darkness. From it came a sound, as if from the depths of time: An echo of a thousand thundering hooves surging out of cave paintings. I saw horses racing toward me. As they left the caves far behind, I saw they pulled chariots, and in the chariots were men armed with lances and javelins and dressed in short tunics.

Then, coming from the east, I saw us, Berber horses. With people on our backs, among them green eyed women in long cloth dresses and colorful jewelry, we spread out into the fertile valleys and green mountains of the vast Maghreb. It stretches from Libya to Morocco, bordered in the north by the glittering Mediterranean Sea.

Next, I heard the sound of waves crashing into the shores of the Berber coast. I saw Phoenician sailors and merchants anchoring their ships at night in the many ports they established, trading unbelievable riches. Thus, out of these riches, I saw the rise of Carthage, city of wonders, of docks surrounded by columns and Greek sculptures. From here I saw the famous man march out with his war elephants and thousands and thousands of us, heading for Rome over the insurmountable Alps. With him, we did the impossible, we did what no one had ever done, nor even dreamed of doing: Crossing those mountains in winter. Oh, Hannibal, what a price we paid. And in the end we didn't conquer Rome. Rather, I had to watch how Rome destroyed beautiful Carthage, not leaving one stone upon another.

And then, with a start, I heard the thundering hooves again. This time all the way from Arabia, carrying the nomadic Bedouins on horses whose beauty was famous all through the Arab lands—horses so precious they slept in their owners' tents and were evacuated before women and children during attacks. But these horses, the drinkers of the wind, didn't stop in the Maghreb. I saw them pour into Spain, into Al-Andalus, where our masters, Moors they are now called, created a hitherto unknown gorgeous creature, the Andalusian horse. This great feat they achieved by mixing the Berber and Arab horses with ancient Spanish blood. Besides, they built mosques and palaces and libraries of medicine and mathematics, and surprisingly, saved the lost knowledge of the classic Greek world.

I saw then the writings on the opened pages of a book from this vanished culture, *De Re Equestri (On Horsemanship)* by Xenophon: "The training should never be harsh, because nothing forced can ever be beautiful." I lost sight of the book and felt the air get cooler as my visions took me far north, to the rulers of the much later Austro-Hungarian empire in Vienna, who bred us Lipizzaners from our cousins, the Andalusians. The empire didn't breed us for hard work, neither for money nor the speed that wins the high stakes at the race courses. Racing may be called the sport of kings, but a Lipizzaner's performance is literally the sport of emperors. We are bred solely for prestige, for strutting in front of nobility. And for this purpose, they built us the Spanish Riding School in Vienna, where they also teach the classical dressage tradition according to the principles of Xenophon.

Then I saw us, hundreds and hundreds of us, frolicking in the fields of Piber, the childhood home of all the horses of the magnificent Spanish Riding School. I saw clearly that we look a bit different from other horses. In our bodies, everything is rounded. There are no sharp angles or bony protuberances, nothing that looks threatening or unpleasant. Our hooves are hard as steel from running around in the Austrian mountain fields during our first three years, but they don't look as if they could harm if they kicked, or that our teeth, underneath that quivering pale muzzle, could sink deep into soft flesh. Looking at us is wanting to touch us, to be helplessly drawn to us like a mother to her baby's soft cheek. Draping our strong muscle and impressive intelligence is our lightness, the color of whipped cream, of rare pleasures, of cooling treats on hot days.

I then saw a dense fog drifting down from the Alpine mountain tops and softly cover the Piber fields. I heard a voice coming out of this white mist and saw a man coming towards me. My whole body was jolted as if stung by lightning when I suddenly recognized the stocky man with a cap and heard what he was saying: "*Heet* him, *heet* him, he plays you!"

I was dreaming. But still, I had heard those words before. Once, many years ago, there was a period when I had been working a lot and felt it was time to take it a bit easier. Margaret didn't want to listen to that, she thought I already had an easy life. Actually, what she said was that I was very good at preserving energy, saving it for when it was absolutely necessary. I am not sure what to think of that. In any event, I developed a discrete cough. It started as a little hacking one day while I was being worked. I had only gotten some dust or a fly in my throat, but the result was surprising: many nice visits to the vet, then off to the veterinary university, more checks and a lot less work. So this day when I stepped into the trailer, I thought it was another pleasant visit to the doctor. We even had a puncture on the way and came in late.

I was a little disappointed to see an arena and not the concerned doctors in white coats, but a stocky man with a cap. It still irks me to think that even then I didn't pay attention. I went into a lazy trot and coughed once. That was when I heard his voice the very first time:

"*Heet* him, *heet* him, he plays you!" And that was also the end of my life as a horse of leisure. His words to dispel my bluff stung more than the light touch of the whip, but Margaret felt as if he had cracked her skull wide open. All she could think afterwards was: "Is this dressage?"

Whatever hard work and training Margaret and I had done together, it was nothing like this. You see, dressage to Margaret was just a necessary routine to reach what she thought were the fun parts of riding: the jumping and the cross country in the three day events. The only reason she went to this lesson was at someone's urging: "You have to ride with the Master when he is in town, you have to, you have a Lipizzaner horse! You owe it to your horse!" After making her decision to go, Margaret of course had to enter unknown terrain with someone she trusted completely, me.

Looking back now, that first lesson was like one of those dreams where events are thrown at you without pause or connections you can see. Creatures appear, impossible situations happen and you just act. In the morning you wake up with a head filled with so much you don't under-stand until you start thinking about it. "In the moment," the Master said, "in the moment." We Lipizzaners, when ridden, react swiftly to what is happening. The rider can't stop and ponder, but has to be in the moment, thus in the movement itself. Just like in a dream.

"Is he a Primavera horse?" The Master then demanded to know, referring to my bloodline. And then, when the Master said he remembered my father, Siglavy Primavera, it was also like a dream. In my life, I had never expected to hear about my father, and certainly not from the Master. He was not a Master yet when he knew my father, but Karl Mikolka, a young bereiter at the Spanish Riding School, where my father was a handsome and very strong stallion. Once when ridden, Father's stirrups banged against the wall and he bucked his rider high into the air. Of course this made him impossible to ride, and instead, with the Master as helper, he was lunged with sandbags on his back. Although this was meant to desensitize him, it only left him in super shape and didn't solve the problem. The next rider to try was also promptly bucked off, this time with no banging stirrups as an excuse. After another two months of lunging, the Master got on him, since he had been assisting the whole time. Father did not buck him off. The Master said he didn't know why, but he did know two lessons that Father had taught him: Never show or indicate fear. It can encourage us to challenge the rider. Furthermore, it is not up to the rider how long it takes to get us relaxed or on the bit. We decide that. Imagine, the Master learning from Father.

After the Master had left the School, he was deeply saddened to hear that Father had foundered. He had been exposed to an ambitious trainer who pushed him too fast. That trainer should have known that he could not be pushed, that everything took twice as long as normal with him. That trainer didn't respect Father. Thus he lost both a good horse and the respect of the Master.

There is a time and a balance to everything. Life with us can easily become unbalanced. To make a living from us takes time and effort and money, and many a horse-person has been abandoned by their loved ones because of this. I can understand that. Myself, I always had an important job in keeping balance in Margaret's life. Since she already had a family when I got her, I took care to see that due attention was given to family life. The best way to do this, I discovered, was to ease her worries. It was necessary for her to be out in the world at competitions and horse shows. That's how she would show us off, and sell us, not me of course, but the others. Seeing how we behaved made people want to put their own horses in training with her, or breed from us, mainly me.

Shows and competitions can be very stressful for people, since they always worry about how their horses are going to behave. Away from home we may suddenly turn into unrecognizable beings who rear or bolt or refuse to move. Anything can happen when horses and people are gathered. So from our very first day I made this a case of trust between us. I would always be calm and well behaved and just do my job. After all, what could possibly upset me after all my years in the circus, with different places, different people, different acts performed around me, never knowing what is around the next corner? There, I really learned to take care of myself and never place myself in a situation where I could fail.

Thus she didn't have to worry about anything before leaving, except for packing. She filled the trailer with saddles and bridles and blankets and boots and hay and picnic baskets, and off we went, she and Greg and their three children and me. I remember so well one outing we had. Greg was not there, so she placed the children on a blanket in the middle of a large green lawn. Margaret and I saw them the whole time we performed, and were prepared to interrupt if they became anxious or restless. But there they sat, perfectly happy in the sun, drinking sodas and munching sandwiches from the picnic basket while they watched us compete.

It pleased me enormously that she trusted me, even left decisions to me. We were partners. Sometimes when she didn't know what to do I took over, and other times I let her decide. Yes, indeed, I always loved family. That's why, when the Master called me a circus horse, as if that was not so good, I forgave him because he praised my beloved offspring and recommended them for sale, and of course because he was Master of Horses.

Yes, I see now, there is a time and a balance to everything. Also to the art of riding. When we have a rider who is balanced, everything is so easy. If the rider's body follows ours, without leaning or tightening, but is loose and poised in body and breath, then the signals we anticipate become almost telepathic and we can do anything.

Margaret and I had many lessons with the Master. She needed me, Siglavy, her best horse when she was learning the old method of training called dressage. Although this was part of my heritage as a Lipizzaner horse, it wasn't easy. Detail had to be added to detail so eventually they became a skill. Not until I mastered the skill could I try to understand the method. This didn't happen in a linear way. Rather, an understanding of a part suddenly appeared, seemingly out of nowhere, like magic, and added itself to the wholeness. Other times an echo from the past was sounding in my very blood and bones and coming forth after slumbering for ages.

The Master was my wizard, revealing that the good rider will feel as if walking with our legs by connecting to our hind leg through dipping the heel so the calf muscles tighten and the leg lengthens, all the while the heel being the lowest point and under the hip. The Master also said dressage is developing our body and mind to the highest degree, creating a thinking equine athlete who moves with fluid, anatomical correctness, power, and grace. That is us. The rider has to learn to ride with a seat that is elegant, effective, and balanced.

But then Tricia left us, and the balance in all life as I knew it was upended. From one day to another, and for the first time in my life, I faced an impossible task: to bring Margaret back into the balance. I didn't know how to do this. And I was scared.

Herd and family life are full of fondness and basking in the routines that make us feel safe. Feedings of grain and hay, and rituals of work sessions followed by grooming and lukewarm showers that rinse off dust and sweat and flies. And overnight all that was gone. Together, we were driven into unknown terrain. I say together, but this was the scariest of all, it wasn't true. We weren't together anymore. I couldn't reach her. For so many years, we had been connected. Now she drifted away from me, towards the other side, where her daughter was.

I had grasped the method of dressage. But it didn't help me now. I needed another method. But I didn't have one. Nor did I have a wizard. I only had a soft nicker when she came to feed me. When she leaned on my neck, I planted my feet on the edge of the abyss where she was lingering and pushed into her so she wouldn't fall in. And when she let me loose into my field, after breakfast, I did what I always did, whinnied loudly and kicked out with my two hind legs, my little freedom celebration.

Every day I turned my head and looked back at her, to see if she smiled at that, as she always did, before. But every time when I looked back, I had already lost her. She didn't look at me. She stared into the abyss.

The seasons changed, from hot to crisp to cold. Nothing else changed.

Then, one morning, I knew the cold season was coming to an end. I smelled the tiny sprouts of new green grass working their way up from the dark soil into the light. I heard the birds singing. The air itself was soft and sweet. When she led me out to my field, her step felt a little lighter. When she let me loose, I ran out and kicked up my hind legs in the pure joy of spring and freedom. As always, I turned my head and looked at her. She looked back at me. I kicked up my hind legs again, stronger this time, and looked at her. She smiled.

Maybe there is a method. A method of time.

Chapter 7

UUUUU

Tuesday September 23

She had moved me to the field beside the outdoor arena where the grass was wet and the young trees lined up, giving some shade. I knew what she was thinking: "Don't upset him, don't change routines, don't make the others jealous, act as if everything is normal." Therefore, as always, she started feeding in the stallion barn before she came to me. She fed me grain from her hand, though. But I couldn't eat. She watched me, waited. She still had a tiny hope: "Will it turn? Which way?"

After she left me and went back to the house, I lowered my neck until my nose touched the grass. It still smelled sweet, but not enough to tempt me to grab it with my teeth and tear it loose. Instead, I bent my front legs until my knees gave out under me, and I allowed myself to fall heavily onto one side.

Although slow waves of pain rolled through me, the grass and the ground under me felt good. I closed my eyes. The air filled with thin threads of noise from birds taking turns weaving intricate patterns in every space above, until I was surrounded by a dome of sound I hadn't heard since my youth, when the circus tent filled with an excited audience: The artists waiting, warmed up, the orchestra starting; one instrument followed by another till the whole soft round-ness of the tent was filled with a web of sound, suddenly crisscrossed by the movements of the flying trapeze artists and the gasping of surprised people.

I thought then I heard the voice of Don, my man, gone for so many years, standing by my side as we waited for the final bell for us to enter the stage. Me, as always, sucking on his collar in that moment of tense anticipation, a little stage fright; they say we true artists always feel that. I flicked my ears to hear his voice better, but it wasn't Don's, only an eagle's scream so far above the other birds I couldn't see it as I tried to lift my head. The effort was too much, I let my head sink.

The herd gathered closer around me, grazing, munching and sighing, letting out breath loudly, shifting weight from one foot to another, nodding off a bit standing in the sun, waking up with a start, maybe from an insect bite. They will keep dangers away from a friend who lays down, except for the flies, they cannot keep them away. They bothered me a bit, but not enough to move, not even an ear now. Tiny bugs crawled under my head, now so heavy on the ground, and into my long mane, always so immaculately brushed and clean, now covering the grass like spun silk. This is the world. It is so close, so shiny and golden, so warm. Underneath it is a silence. All I want to do is to reach that quiet place, to be left in peace, to be undisturbed.

But then, suddenly, a new kind of pain takes hold, not slow rolling in and then fading out like before.

No, it stays, with claws deep inside me that hold and rip, spreading through my body, following the veins and the bones out into my very limbs. I try to move away from it, but I can't move my body, only my head. I keep pressing my head into the ground, which firmly resists me.

The soothing sounds from the herd fade. Instead I hear the soft padding of the paws of the big black cats. They are coming from that deep dark hole that I now know awaits me, that well of dark mulch, of worms, and creatures without eyes. Out of that abyss the black cats rise, ready to tear and rip pieces of us while we still help-lessly breathe.

I can't run, I can't kick, I can't even lift my head or open my mouth in a stallion's coarse scream. But from inside me, from the bottom of what is me, from beyond everything I have known till now, I cry out. I cry out for her, and I beg: "Don't leave me. Don't leave me here alone."

The sudden silence that opens up then fills with sighing and snorting and shuffling from my herd. In the air the eagle screams again. I listen for the padding of the paws of the black cats but now I can't hear them. Instead, other footsteps are coming closer, stopping, then turning and quickening towards the house. The door of the house opens and then, now that she has been told: Her footsteps, closer and closer.

With a sigh and with the pain gone, I open my eyes and I see her so clearly, so close, as never before. Little things now loom so big: Her smile every time she let me loose in my field after work, and I would nicker loud and kick out hard with my hind legs in the exuberant joy of being free. Her whispers in my ear when trying new things, like jumping: "Come on, you can do it!"

Again, the day is golden, and shiny, like the days of our life together, when we became more in each other's presence than we could be on our own. Neither man nor animal, but a new creature; since for man to peer into the soul of animal is to see deeper into himself, and for man to blend with the body of animal is to move above earth with the strength of angels.

And in that moment I see that the big cats that followed me in my life were never there, except only that one night so long ago in the circus, when I was trapped in my stall with the runaway black panther. The others were only shadows in my mind. They are gone. They never were. But she is there. Here. She is here.

Then her voice, gently prodding me: "Come on my boy, are you having a wee nap?"

Still, I can't get up. I don't want to. What would hurt most would be to get up, to move around, to not be quiet, to not lie down. I press my face harder into the ground.

But then the little dog, the house pet, suddenly scurries out from the house and lies down beside me, her back to mine, pressing against me, her little head facing the opposite way of my head and buried between her front paws.

Above me, and still above the bird song, the eagle's screams are getting louder. A longing comes into me. I, who always carried others, long now to have the eagle's wings, to jump but not to land on hard ground again, to leap but not come down, to float, in his spirit, not in these heavy matters of the flesh.

I hear Margaret talking on the phone, an urgency buried deep beneath the calm of her voice.

I was still lying down. But she didn't have to prod me again. As we both waited for the last bit of strength to bring me up on my legs again, she quietly leaned down and stroked my head. I knew by now she was going to help me go. She was going to release me. She was loyal to me. She always was.

I got up.

I have to admit, I got a little confused at that point and wanted to go down again. But she understood and leaned her weight into me to support me, again whispering in my ear during our walk: "Come on, you can do it!" I knew where we were going, to the field behind the barn, at the highest end of the property.

I was still standing when the vet came and listened to my gut sound. Then I lay down. I managed to bend my knees and lower myself over to the side quite gracefully this time, despite my vanishing strength. Again, the dog came over and lay down beside me, in the same way, back to back, little head between paws. Soft and soothing voices mingled with the bird song, everybody's steps were slow and gentle in their doing what they had to do now.

Then I saw the eagle, first hovering high above, then coming closer and soaring around the trees next to the house. He was huge. I saw the white head and tail as he circled around before heading straight towards me. Then he circled again around the closest tree, slowly, looking down at all of us, coming to bring me to that place between holding on and letting go. It belongs to everyone, and is everywhere. In that place your past is gone and the future is not yet there. In the same moment the past is present together with the future. It is so quiet that from there you can see it all at once:

I see the white head of the eagle, I see me and Mara, standing together, admiring our first foal. I see Margaret, laughing with her daughter. I hear the swoosh of the eagle's wings and I see me nudging Margaret to step into the morning, into the light after the long night of the loss of the child. I look into the eyes of the eagle and I see Margaret as she plants the third tree in late September. My tree, on the highest point of the property, besides Mara and Missi, my mares.

Margaret's face is so close now, and behind her, the eagle hovering a few feet over me. I try to get up. I can't hear her words over the beatings of the eagle's wings. But when I feel her warm breath into my ear, "Come on, you can do it," I nicker and kick out hard with my hind legs, like always when let loose, trying to reach the eagle. When his wings touch me, her breath and her words still linger in my ear.

Then, as I let my breath go and quietly sink down, the wings of the eagle embrace me. I become the rider, not the ridden. And I feel as if all is new again, as the rider feels on a horse mounted for the first time. Honored and humble, carried by such strength and innocence.

And then, you just go. Just like that. You just go. As we Masters say: Like so.

Afterword

On a clear night the following spring, both Margaret and Greg were awakened by hooves trotting past the house and onto the asphalt road along the property. They rushed out, each with a flashlight, but no horse was to be seen, only the sound of trotting hooves.

Greg took off in the car down the road, Margaret went into the barn to see which horse was missing. They were all there, sleepy-headed and surprised by a visit in the night.

She looked everywhere before she went back to the house, puzzled. Inside the house, she heard the horse return, now coming from the road and passing the house on the way to the barn.

Excited, she ran outside to catch it as Greg came back in the car:

"Greg, he's back, did you chase him up the road and in?"

"No, I didn't see any horse out front!"

Margaret stood under the stars, in the quiet of the night, looking towards the three trees silhouetted against the spring sky, and realized that the sound of the trotting hooves had been from a horse shod only on the front legs:

"Siglavy," she whispered. She shook her head and went inside.

Siglavy Sagana II
Photo by Sally Barnett, 1983

Siglavy Sagana II

UUUUU

Siglavy Sagana II was born in 1972 and grew up at the sprawling El Capitan Ranch near Santa Barbara, California. El Capitan imported horses from the Spanish Riding School in Vienna to the United States. As a three-year-old, Siglavy was sold to Don McLennan, who had been the head trainer at the San Diego Zoo as well as an animal trainer for the movie, Dr. Doolittle.

Don had an animal training center in Grants Pass, Oregon, where he trained animals exclusively for the circus. Siglavy was his lead stallion in a liberty act of three stallions. While under McLennan's training, Siglavy appeared in Circus Vargas and the Ringling Brothers Circus, among others. However, when Siglavy was nine years old, Don got sick and had to sell off his horses.

When Greg Gill visited McLennan's farm to look at some training equipment; Don showed Siglavy to him and told him to bring back his wife Margaret to see the horse. After the subsequent meeting, Siglavy returned with Margaret and Greg to Highland Stables in Beaver Creek, Oregon, where he embarked on a new and varied career, including eventing and being an ambassador for the Lipizzaner breed. At one such occasion, the multi-talented stallion competed in dressage one day, and the following day showed in the exhibition class, where he demonstrated stunts he performed during his show-business days.

Siglavy also became a mentor to Margaret, deeply influencing her life. He lived with Margaret and Greg Gill at Highland Stables till the end of his days, living to be 31 years old.

Margaret Gill

 ∪ ∪ ∪ ∪ ∪ ∪

Margaret Gill began her education with horses at the age of twelve in Scotland with Robert Young, FBHS, British Pony Club and British Horse Society. She immigrated to Ontario, Canada where she met her husband, Greg. They settled in Oregon, where they still live today.

Margaret's training continued in Oregon with Mike Pereillo Jr., Erik Herbermann, and Karl Mikolka. Her latest venture with horses led her to become an Equine Specialist for Equine Assisted Growth and Learning Association (Eagala). Presently she enjoys working with some of Siglavy's offspring and riding his grandson Siglavy II Calista.

Lisbeth Asay

UUUUU

While waiting to turn ten, the age required to join the riders, Lisbeth Asay watched her seniors and their horses trot around the outdoor arena at the riding school. When her day to ride finally arrived, it was on Coq d'Or, nicknamed Coggen, a former race horse, that she made her 'debut.' She loved him from the first time he turned his head and snapped his teeth or left her lying in the ice-cold mud gazing up at him trotting away. And then, at last, riding Coggen at the canter, knowing he didn't do this for free and he didn't do it for just anyone.

Much later, Lisbeth had a career in newspapers, publishing houses and schools in Norway, but the horses were never forgotten. She became part of the majority of horse lovers in the world—all those who love horses but don't own them.

Lisbeth Asay lives in Portland with her husband. After moving there from Norway, and realizing it was horse heaven, she looked for a Quarter Horse to lease for trail riding. Instead, she stumbled upon Seri, and without planning on it, acquired her own horse, a mature Dutch

Warmblood, of good breeding but with a checkered past. As with Coq d'Or, love was instant but not mild and mellow.

Lisbeth sought out Margaret Gill at Highland Stables to help with her Seri. One day, when Margaret asked Lisbeth if she would be interested in writing a book about her Lipizzaner stallion, horses and writing joined forces to create *I, Siglavy*.

XENOPHON PRESS LIBRARY
www.XenophonPress.com

Xenophon Press is dedicated to the preservation of classical equestrian literature. We bring both new and old works to English-speaking riders.

30 Years with Master Nuno Oliveira, Henriquet 2011

A New Method to Dress Horses, Cavendish 2018

A Rider's Survival from Tyranny, de Kunffy 2012

Another Horsemanship, Racinet 1994

Austrian Art of Riding, Poscharnigg 2015

Classic Show Jumping: the de Nemethy Method, de Nemethy 2016

Divide and Conquer Book 1, Lemaire de Ruffieu 2016

Divide and Conquer Book 2, Lemaire de Ruffieu 2017

Dressage for the 21st Century, Belasik 2001

Dressage in the French Tradition, Diogo de Bragança 2011

Dressage Principles and Techniques, Tavora 2017

Dressage Principles Illuminated, Expanded Edition, de Kunffy 2017

École de Cavalerie Part II, Robichon de la Guérinière 1992, 2015

Equine Osteopathy: What the Horses Have Told Me, Giniaux 2014

Fragments from the writings of Max Ritter von Weyrother, Fane 2017

François Baucher: The Man and His Method, Baucher/Nelson 2013

Great Horsewomen of the 19th Century in the Circus, Nelson 2015

Gymnastic Exercises for Horses Volume II, Eleanor Russell 2013

H. Dv. 12 Cavalry Manual of Horsemanship, Reinhold 2014

Handbook of Jumping Essentials, Lemaire de Ruffieu 2015

Handbook of Riding Essentials, Lemaire de Ruffieu 2015

Healing Hands, Giniaux, DVM 1998

Horse Training: Outdoors and High School, Beudant 2014

I, Siglavy, Asay 2018

Learning to Ride, Santini 2016

Legacy of Master Nuno Oliveira, Millham 2013

Lessons in Lightness, Mark Russell 2016

Methodical Dressage of the Riding Horse, Faverot de Kerbrech 2010

Principles of Dressage and Equitation, a.k.a. Breaking and Riding, Fillis 2017

Racinet Explains Baucher, Racinet 1997

Science and Art of Riding in Lightness, Stodulka 2015

The Art of Riding a Horse or Description of Modern Manége in Its Perfection, D'Eisenberg 2015

The Art of Traditional Dressage, Volume I DVD, de Kunffy 2013

The Ethics and Passions of Dressage Expanded Ed., de Kunffy 2013

The Forward Impulse, Santini 2016

The Gymnasium of the Horse, Steinbrecht 2011

The Horses, a novel, Elaine Walker 2015

The Italian Tradition of Equestrian Art, Tomassini 2014

The Maneige Royal, de Pluvinel 2010, 2015

The Portuguese School of Equestrian Art, de Oliveira/da Costa 2012

The Spanish Riding School & Piaffe and Passage, Decarpentry 2013

To Amaze the People with Pleasure and Delight, Walker 2015

Total Horsemanship, Racinet 1999

Training with Master Nuno Oliveira double DVD set, Eleanor Russell 2016

Truth in the Teaching of Master Nuno Oliveira, Eleanor Russell 2015

Wisdom of Master Nuno Oliveira, de Coux 2012

Available at www.XenophonPress.com